Look out for more adventures from

Collect them all!

1 ☐ **DRAGON RIDER**
2 ☐ **SELKIE WARRIOR**

☐ **THE DEEP: THE OFFICIAL HANDBOOK**
☐ **THE DEEP: STICKER ACTIVITY BOOK**

DRAGON RIDER

FINN BLACK

BLOOMSBURY
CHILDREN'S BOOKS

LONDON OXFORD NEW YORK NEW DELHI SYDNEY

With special thanks to Speckled Pen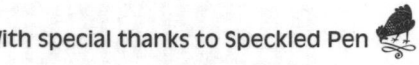

BLOOMSBURY CHILDREN'S BOOKS
Bloomsbury Publishing Plc
50 Bedford Square, London WC1B 3DP, UK

BLOOMSBURY, BLOOMSBURY CHILDREN'S BOOKS and the Diana logo
are trademarks of Bloomsbury Publishing Plc

First published in Great Britain in 2018 by Bloomsbury Publishing Plc

These books are based on the multi-award-winning television series The Deep,
produced by DHX Media and A Stark Production. Technicolor Creative Services
is the primary rights holder. The Deep series is based on the original graphic
novels created by Tom Taylor and James Brouwer

A catalogue record for this book is available from the British Library

ISBN: PB: 978-1-4088-9874-1; eBook: 978-1-4088-9873-4

2 4 6 8 10 9 7 5 3 1

Printed and bound in Great Britain by CPI Group (UK) Ltd, Croydon CR0 4YY

MIX
Paper from
responsible sources
FSC® C020471

To find out more about our authors and books visit www.bloomsbury.com
and sign up for our newsletters

With special thanks to Dan Metcalf and David Shephard,
along with Steven Wendland and Marty Kossoff.

With additional thanks to Alison Warner, Pam Kunick-Cohen,
Avrill Stark, Robert Chandler, Tom Taylor, James Brouwer,
Wolfgang Bylsma, Trent Carlson, Kirsten Newlands, Anne Loi,
Rob Spindley, Logan McPherson, Sophie Bloomfield,
and John Lomas-Bullivant.

PROLOGUE

'**C**ome on, Jeffrey! Last one there's a blobfish!'
Ant Nekton zoomed through the ocean in the Shadow Knight, the sleek, high-tech underwater exploration suit he used for missions. Beside his visor, he could see Jeffrey, his pet fish – and best friend – flapping his fins furiously to keep up, but the Shadow Knight was too fast for him. Ant steered the suit down to the sea bed and away from the

Aronnax, the giant submarine that the Nekton family called home, which floated above them like a huge metal whale.

Ant had convinced his parents, Will and Kaiko, to let him explore the nearby kelp forests. As a junior explorer, he knew that the kelp forests were often used by organisms as a safe place to hide from predators. Ant was always on the lookout for new discoveries, whether it was a strange species of sea snail, or something more exciting ...

As he approached the forest he cut the Knight's engines so that the vibrations fell to a low hum. He didn't want to disturb any forms of sea life living there. He felt his heart give a nervous flutter. There was no telling what he might find in the depths of the ocean ...

'OK, what do we have today?' he muttered. Jeffrey finally caught up and swam next to Ant, his eyes bulging from the effort. If a fish could pant for breath, that's what Jeffrey would have been doing. Ant reached out the Knight's mechanical hands to part the swaying column of kelp and peered between the strands. 'Kelp ... kelp ... and more kelp. Hmm, I was hoping for something a little less ... *kelpy*.'

They investigated a little further and found nothing more than a strangely coloured piece of algae, but then Jeffrey darted off towards a hidden corner of the forest.

'Jeffrey? What is it? Have you found something?'

Ant followed his little orange and purple fish to a mound of sand and looked closely at it.

'Seems like it's just a heap of sand,' he said to his faithful fish. 'Come on, let's go back to – *Whoa*!'

A sudden swell of current buffeted the Shadow Knight and caused the kelp forest to sway. Grain by grain, the sand mound in front of them drifted away to reveal a strange, ancient-looking object beneath the surface.

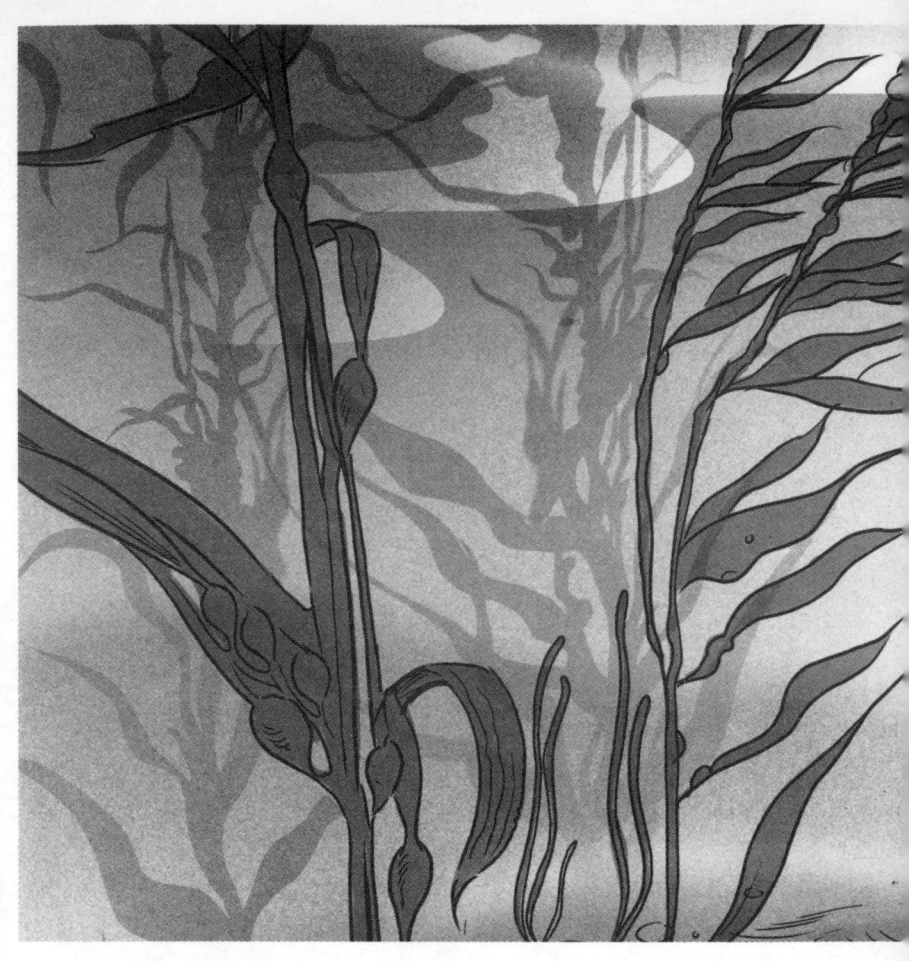

Ant felt his eyes grow wide and his skin
prickle. 'What. Is. *That?!*'

He carefully brushed away the rest of the
sand to reveal a round metal object the size
of a cricket ball. It was a dirty green, the

colour of an old, unpolished penny. Around
the centre of the sphere was a protruding
ring, and it was covered in barnacle shells,
just as most things were under the sea
when they had been there for a long time.

But how long? Something about the look of it made Ant think it had been there for centuries.

Slowly, he lifted the orb out of its resting place and instantly felt a shiver of excitement run down his body. Jeffrey danced around him.

'It could be anything.' Ant shrugged. 'Maybe just a piece of sea junk, or something someone dropped off the side of their boat years ago.' He glanced at Jeffrey and burst out in a grin. 'Who am I kidding? I have no idea what this is, but it's definitely *awesome*!'

It wasn't every day that Ant came across buried treasure in a kelp forest.

He held it gently in his mechanical grip and powered up the Shadow Knight. He turned to head back to the Aronnax, where he would be able to investigate properly.

'Jeffrey, old pal, I have a feeling life in the ocean just became even *more* interesting ...'

A column of bubbles erupted from the little fish as he mouthed his agreement.

The two of them headed home. This discovery was something they *had* to share ... when Ant was ready.

CHAPTER ONE

'**Y**ou guys are not going to *believe* this!'

Ant carried his mystery object across the bridge of the Aronnax. The orb was covered with an old dust sheet. He'd managed to keep his discovery a secret from the rest of the Nektons for an entire two weeks while he'd worked on it. None of them had any idea it even existed.

It was nearly dusk and the family had just

returned from a talk Kaiko had given at the Tokyo University of Marine Science. Everyone, that is, except Ant, who had stayed behind to prepare his surprise. Ant loved visiting new places but, having grown up on a submarine, being on solid land felt peculiar to him. There wasn't the usual hum of engines and swaying movement that he was so used to on the Aronnax.

Ant carefully placed the strange object on a control panel.

'So what have we got here, Ant?' asked Will. The Nektons gathered round, used to 'Ant's hobby of creating imaginative (and occasionally unsuccessful) inventions.

'You remember that I went exploring in the kelp forests a while ago?' he began, looking from face to face. He paused for dramatic effect. 'I found something!'

'Would that "something" be the reason you stayed back on board the Aronnax these past couple of weeks?' said Kaiko with a smile and a raised eyebrow. 'I thought you said you were staying behind to "guard" the Aronnax?'

'Um, I was kind of doing both?' said Ant with a sheepish grin. 'I've been working on restoring my "something" to its former glory. And now I want you all to see it!'

'Can't this wait, son?' yawned Will. 'I think we're all pretty beat from your mother's talk at the university – which was excellent, by the way, dear!'

'Thank you!' smiled Kaiko, folding her arms. 'Good to know I didn't bore you to sleep.'

'What is so important that it has to keep me from my bed?' said Ant's sister, Fontaine, giving him a level stare.

'Trust me,' said Ant, 'this'll be worth it.'

The family looked on in anticipation.

'Ladies and gentlemen! And you, Fontaine! I am pleased to finally unveil the latest of my amazing, mind-boggling, awe-inducing discoveries!' Ant performed a drum roll on his tummy. 'I call it – the CIRCLOTRON!'

He whipped the dust sheet away to reveal the strange-looking contraption he had saved from the sea bed. Since recovering it, Ant had lovingly cleaned it and carefully brushed away the mud of hundreds, maybe thousands of years, so that it was now a tarnished brown colour.

'The ... *Circlotron*?' said Fontaine, peering at it.

'Yeah!'

'Seriously?'

'Yeah, seriously!' said Ant, affronted. 'It didn't have a name, so Jeffrey and I came up with one. Cool, huh?'

Fontaine rolled her eyes.

'I'm going to bed,' she said, turning to leave.

'Wait a second, Fontaine,' said Will. He moved closer to inspect the unusual device.

'Your brother may have something here. What does it do, Ant?'

'Do?' said Ant. 'Um ... I haven't got a clue! But that's the fun part about science, right? Finding out about stuff?'

'It certainly is,' said Kaiko, peering at the Circlotron. 'What are those markings?' She traced her fingers over a few engravings on the ring that ran around the centre of the globe.

'They're glyphs. Lemurian, wouldn't you say, Dad?' said Ant.

Will grinned as he examined the Circlotron more closely. 'If this is a Lemurian artefact, then it is incredibly exciting.'

'Look – just yesterday I cleared away some impacted sand and I found this hole in the side.' Ant angled the Circlotron so that the others could see a tiny hole, hidden beneath the ring. 'I think it might be a keyhole. Maybe it's mechanical, like clockwork?'

'And you want to wind it up?' said Fontaine.

'It could be anything! A crazy, mechanical cricket ball! A weird robot-fish egg!'

'*Or* it could be the next clue to discovering the ancient city of Lemuria! What do you think, Dad?' Ant looked at Will hopefully.

Will donned his reading glasses to look at the symbols and walked around the Circlotron for a few moments, stroking his chin in thought. Will had dedicated his entire life to researching the lost, ancient civilisation of Lemuria, and no one knew more on the subject than him.

'The symbols are definitely Lemurian,' he admitted. 'Are you sure this is going to work, Ant?'

'Come on, Dad! When has anything I've done ever gone wrong?' said Ant. Will drew breath to speak. 'Actually, don't answer that! This is *totally* going to work.'

Will and Kaiko looked at each other and shrugged.

'Let's do it!'

Will fetched some tools and managed to bend a piece of metal to fit the shape of the keyhole. Ant scooped up the Circlotron into the palm of his hand. Then, shaking with excitement, he took the key and slid it into the Circlotron. He turned it and to his surprise there was no resistance – it smoothly went round. From deep inside the Circlotron they could hear a series of whirrs and cracks and clicks. Cogs which had laid unused for centuries began to move. He felt a judder travel through his hand as the device buzzed into life.

'Nektons,' said Ant with an air of drama, 'meet the Circlotron.' The ball hummed and whirred and suddenly a shaft of white light shot out from the top, making Ant almost drop it – almost.

'Whoa!' said Fontaine.

'Yes! It worked!' Ant held out the Circlotron.

He could feel its energy pulsing through him. Will and Kaiko moved out of the way of the beam, shielding their eyes.

'Aargh! Put it down!' shouted Fontaine, dazzled by the light. 'Did you find an ancient Lemurian flashlight?'

'What? No! Whatever this is, it's *way* more important than a flashlight.' Ant placed the Circlotron carefully on the floor. The light seemed to settle and point upwards, through the observation window and into the night sky. The beam moved wildly west to east.

'Really? Because it looks like a flashlight,' said Fontaine, not even trying to hide a yawn. 'I'll be in my room ...'

Ant stared at the light and the path it cut into the sky. Whatever this was, he knew it was essential to understanding the Lemurians. He could feel it in his bones. He looked up at the light and tried to track where the line was pointing. Suddenly –

'Oh. Oh, whoa! I think ... I think I know ...' Ant stumbled over his words as a hundred thoughts hit him at once. 'I think I know what it does!'

Still holding the Circlotron in the palm of his hand, Ant rushed to a control panel to note down the current coordinates of the Aronnax and started to do some mental calculations. He grabbed a tablet computer and brought up a map of their position. *Yes!* he thought. *It fits!*

As the beam of light moved, it was drawing a straight line through the black pit of space, highlighting several stars along its path. 'I've got it! We're travelling towards the equator, which is to the south, here,' he said, pointing to the on-screen map. 'Look at the line the light is pointing to. The Circlotron must be tracking the *celestial* equator!'

'Remarkable,' said Will.

'You're right! Very clever, Ant!' said Kaiko.

She gave her son a hug. Fontaine looked at her family and shrugged.

'I don't get it,' she said. 'What's the big deal?'

'It's –' began Will.

'Dad, allow me,' said Ant with a grin. 'I don't mind explaining to my sister.'

Fontaine rolled her eyes, but she was listening.

Ant paced across the floor as he explained. 'The celestial equator is just like it says. The equator is an imaginary line around the middle of the Earth, right? Well, the *celestial* equator is an imaginary line across the night sky.'

'Er ... right,' said Fontaine.

'Say you got a rubber band and stretched it around the world,' he said.

'That's a pretty *big* rubber band!' Fontaine laughed.

'Well, if you keep stretching it outwards,

that's the celestial equator. The Circlotron is tracking it and projecting it on to the sky. Look!' Ant pointed to the bright beam of light. 'See how that glowing white line runs through the constellations? Right above us, the line goes straight through Mintaka – the rightmost star in Orion's Belt!'

Fontaine nodded, finally grasping the concept.

'I ... I *suppose* that's pretty cool ...' she mumbled. Ant leaped up again and Will ruffled his hair.

'Good job, son,' he said. 'You've been studying the stars, haven't you?'

'A little,' Ant shrugged modestly. In truth, he had been reading up on constellations and astronomy for months. 'I just thought that the more I understood about how the skies and the oceans connect, the closer we might get to discovering where Lemuria is located.'

'Great thinking,' nodded Will. 'After all, we know that the ancient Lemurians used the stars as their guide across the seas. It could be that the Circlotron – *love* the name, by the way – is an ancient piece of Lemurian maritime equipment.'

Ant smiled. Finding the lost city of Lemuria was the Nekton family's mission, and Ant loved doing anything he could to help. He stared into the night sky, daydreaming about finally finding Lemuria. He was smugly congratulating himself on his discovery when –

WOOP WOOP WOOP!

The shrill sound made Ant jump. A call was coming through, the Aronnax's monitors flashing red. He placed the Circlotron back down and the whirring sound from within stopped. The cogs inside ground to a halt and the light faded. Ant went to his position on the bridge, where Kaiko and Will were already in their seats.

'It's an emergency call from the Worldwide Oceanic Association!' said Will. 'They need our help – now!'

CHAPTER TWO

The image of a stern-looking woman in uniform flashed up on the Aronnax's monitors.

'Commander Pyrosome, how can we help?' said Kaiko.

'We're picking up a disturbance in the South China Sea, just off the Paracel Islands,' said the commander.

'What's the problem?' asked Will.

'The WOA has been monitoring the area and we think we've detected a weakness in the Earth's crust there. Magma has been erupting from the ocean floor,' said Commander Pyrosome.

'Like an underwater volcano?' said Ant. He almost leaped out of his seat in excitement. 'Cool!'

'Absolutely *not* cool,' said Pyrosome sternly. Ant sat back down, feeling like he'd just been told off by a teacher. 'The leaking magma is sending poisonous magmatic gas into the sea. As you can imagine, along with the boiling seawater, this is not good for the creatures that live there.'

She pressed a button on her screen and a map popped up on the Aronnax's monitors. She used the computer to draw a line along the map and circle a dark blue blob.

'I've been monitoring the eruptions and they seem to be travelling along the weak

line of the Earth's crust. They are getting perilously close to this area –' she tapped her fingertip against the screen – 'which is vitally important to our research. It houses fossils and organisms that are one of a kind. It's a blue hole known as the Dragon Hole.'

'Dragons?' said Ant. He straightened up, exchanging an excited glance with Jeffrey, who was in his mounted fishbowl, eagerly watching the action on the screen.

'It's just a name, Ant,' said Fontaine. Ant sighed with disappointment.

'As the Aronnax is the closest vessel to the area …' Commander Pyrosome said, her eyes glittering. 'The Association had hoped …'

'We can't set off before morning,' said Will, guessing what her question was going to be. He rubbed his eyes and yawned. Commander Pyrosome looked less than happy – she was used to getting her own way.

'Will, Kaiko, this is serious,' she said. 'There

could be much more at stake than we realise. I need you to investigate ... *now*.'

Will and Kaiko exchanged a glance.

'Commander, I'd like to remind you that the Nektons don't work for the WOA,' said Kaiko. Her face had hardened, like when she was telling Ant to clean up his room.

'Which is why you would be doing us a massive favour,' said Pyrosome. 'As well as managing a potentially dangerous situation for the ocean of course.'

There was a moment's silence. Ant looked at his parents. *Please let them say yes!* He'd give anything to visit the Dragon Hole – it just sounded so mystical, so legendary, so ... dragon-ey.

'It's a dangerous journey to take by night,' said Kaiko, glancing at her controls. 'But I don't think we have a choice right now, if this is so urgent.'

'Thank you. I'll send over the coordinates,' said Commander Pyrosome. 'It's vital that you control the explosions near the sinkhole. It could spell disaster for the sea life in that area. Over and out.'

Fontaine groaned.

'We're going on a mission? Now?'

Ant ran over to his dad. 'Hey, how about we travel like the Lemurians? We can use the Circlotron and have stars as our guide, just like the ancient sailors!'

'Sure,' said Fontaine dryly. 'Or how about we use *technology*. Like all the equipment we have *right here*? Just a thought ...'

'Aw, Dad!' Ant started to complain.

'Your sister's right,' said Will. 'We don't yet know enough about how the Lemurians used the Circlotron. Let's play it safe and get there as quickly as we can.'

'Thank you!' said Fontaine. 'Plotting co-ordinates now.' She tapped on her control panel and a series of numbers came up on the monitor, followed by a satellite image of the area they were heading towards.

'Full power ahead!' said Kaiko. The Aronnax's engines throbbed from deep inside the vessel, and the submarine moved forwards, picking up speed until they were darting through the sea. It never stopped being exciting, no matter how many times they'd sliced through the ocean.

Ant peered through the observation window at the front of the sub, enjoying the experience of watching the underwater environment at night-time. With only the Aronnax's lights to cut through the darkness, the marine world looked like an entirely different place to the one Ant knew so well. Plants, fish and squid appeared more eerie somehow.

They sailed through the night, sleeping in shifts.

When Ant awoke in the morning, Will, Kaiko and Fontaine were already on the bridge. Ant stopped by the study on his way there and started reading one of the old leather-bound, dusty books. There was something he wanted to check.

'Morning, guys!' he said when he joined his family on the bridge. 'Did you know that –'

'Here we go,' said Fontaine. 'Welcome to Ant's fun facts! Every time we head somewhere new, you break out the guidebooks.'

'What?' said Ant, pretending to look hurt. He knew his sister was only teasing. 'I just wanted to look into the history a little more. I mean, it can't be called the "Dragon Hole" for nothing, right?'

'Dragons don't exist, Ant!' Fontaine said, as if talking to a three-year-old.

'Go ahead, son,' Will said. 'What did you learn?'

'Did you know that the South China Sea is famous for its blue holes? The Dragon Hole is the largest one in the world! It's one hundred and twenty-six metres wide, and three hundred metres deep. It holds one hundred and twenty species of fish and –'

'Dragons?' teased Fontaine.

'Ha ha. I did look up ocean dragons, even though they absolutely and *totally* don't exist,' Ant said, winking at Jeffrey. 'There used to be something called "sea dragons", back in the times of the dinosaurs. They were called plesiosaurs. Not dinosaurs exactly, but still – really ancient marine reptiles.'

'And like dinosaurs, completely and utterly extinct,' said Fontaine.

'I know that!' said Ant. 'Dad, did you know you had a book about them in your library, called *The Book of the Great Sea Dragons*? It has these amazing drawings and –'

SHUNK!

Ant and his family were thrown forwards in their seats as the Aronnax gave a sudden lurch.

'What on earth … ?' said Will.

Fontaine checked a control monitor that was flashing red. 'We've caught one of the propellers on something. Putting it up on screen now.'

She pressed a few buttons and the observation screen showed an image from the rear of the submarine. The starboard-side propeller was snagged on what looked like a large net that spread out around the area behind them.

'A net? There's not supposed to be any fishing in this area,' said Kaiko. 'What's it attached to?'

Fontaine pressed another button and the camera zoomed in slowly to a dark shape in the background. As the image became clear, Ant recognised it instantly. It was a mean-looking rust bucket of a submarine.

Just a few lights beamed from its portholes, but Ant could still make out the white skull and crossbones painted on its hull.

'Pirates!' he whispered.

'Captain Hammerhead. I might have known,' said Kaiko. Her eyes narrowed and her nostrils flared. She spoke through clenched teeth, barely containing her anger. 'Will someone please go and cut us free?'

Ant and Fontaine looked at each other and leaped up at the same time.

'We'll go!'

CHAPTER THREE

They raced away from the bridge and down to the Moon Pool, Ant scooping up his Circlotron. He struggled to strap the Jorange, Jeffrey's portable fish tank, on to his back and carry the Circlotron at the same time.

Fontaine was a few strides ahead of him and dived into the pilot's seat of the Rover, the tiny submarine they used to get to the places the Aronnax couldn't go. It had two clawed arms attached to the front, perfect for cutting through pirate nets.

'Aw, come on, Fontaine! You always get to be pilot!' moaned Ant.

'For several good reasons.' She smiled as she ran through a checklist in the cockpit. 'One: I got here first. Two: I'm a better pilot and have never crashed the Rover into the sea bed.'

'I did that *one time*!' said Ant.

'And three: I'm the oldest. Are you coming or not?'

Ant begrudgingly sat in the co-pilot's seat and put the Circlotron into the footwell of the cockpit.

'What are you bringing that for?' asked Fontaine.

'It's my discovery,' said Ant, stroking it protectively. 'Wherever *I* go, *it* goes.'

Fontaine sighed. 'Are you sure that's a good idea?' But Ant didn't respond.

The reinforced glass canopy descended over them, sealing them into the vehicle. A robotic arm clamped on to the top of the Rover and lowered them into the Moon Pool, a circular entrance in the sub that led into the wide ocean. Jeffrey peered through the glass and out into the ocean with a look of wonder on his face. At least, Ant *assumed* it was a look of wonder – if he was being honest with himself, Jeffrey's facial expressions were all very similar.

'If you get to be the pilot, I get to work the cutters,' said Ant. 'Deal?'

'OK. Let's just get this done so we can get back to the real mission.'

The Rover emerged into the water outside the Aronnax and Fontaine deftly moved it around to the stern of the giant submarine. There they saw that the net caught on their propeller was drifting out behind the Dark Orca, Captain Hammerhead's pirate sub.

'What are they doing? I've never known the pirates to fish before,' said Fontaine. 'The net is huge!'

'Maybe they're hunting for plesiosaurs, like we are?' smiled Ant. Fontaine groaned and lowered the craft closer to the net.

'OK, li'l bro,' she said. 'Snip away.'

Ant looked closely at the controls.

'Hmm, looks like the net is made of strong stuff,' he muttered. 'Time to get that laser working!'

Ant used the controls just like he was playing a computer game, steering the Rover's claws into position and readying the laser cutter.

'Ready ... aim ... fire!'

The red beam shot out of the claws and sliced through the net like it was soggy spaghetti. Jeffrey bobbed inside his Jorange.

'Hmm? What's that Jeffrey?' said Ant. 'Awesome firing skills? Why, thank you!'

'We're free,' said Kaiko's voice over the radio. 'You can head back home now.'

'OK,' said Fontaine. Suddenly the controls in the Rover started to emit a loud blip. 'Wait! There's something else caught in the net.'

She steered them away from the Aronnax and over to the Dark Orca. As they moved closer to the net near the hull of the submarine, Ant saw what their monitors had found. Twisted in the net was a beautiful, blue, bottle-nosed dolphin.

'Aw! Hey little guy!' said Ant. 'Don't worry, we'll get you out in no time.'

'Be careful,' said Kaiko's voice. 'I don't like how close you are to the Dark Orca. We can't trust Captain Hammerhead.'

Fontaine checked the controls.

'I don't think they've seen us,' she said. 'We'll just free this dolphin and get back home. Cut him loose, Ant.'

Ant manoeuvred the arms of the Rover,

but it was clear that to cut the net near the dolphin's tail would be a delicate operation. He couldn't use the laser again – it was too dangerous. Luckily the end of each arm was equipped with three finger-like appendages for more intricate tasks. He extended them and the dolphin began to thrash about.

'Whoa, easy!' said Ant soothingly. His eyes met the dolphin's through the glass of the Rover and the dolphin seemed to calm. It took a few tense minutes, but Ant finally cut the net free and the dolphin swam away happily. 'See ya!' called Ant.

'Heading back to the Aronnax now – Aargh!' shouted Fontaine. The Rover rocked and they looked up to see that a giant claw extending out from the Dark Orca had clamped on to them. 'OK, they've definitely seen us now!'

The claw dragged them up to the surface of the Dark Orca's Moon Pool and they found themselves in the centre of the pirate sub.

It was a world away from the Aronnax. The Nektons' sub was clean, white and state of the art, but Hammerhead's was sludgy brown, dark and full of rusty salvage. Thankfully, there didn't seem to be anyone around. The claw let go of the Nektons' Rover just as the outer hatch to the Moon Pool closed, shutting off their only way of escaping.

'What the … ?' Ant muttered. 'Maybe we can open the hatch again and get out of here.'

'OK, quick, before someone comes,' said Fontaine. They climbed out of the Rover.

They walked out on to the platform, searching for the hatch release lever.

'It's got to be here somewhere. Maybe it's – Aargh!'

Ant was suddenly jerked backwards and

felt the Jorange being wrestled from him. He fell to the floor and saw Jeffrey being dangled from a mechanical claw.

'Hey!' Ant called, alarm darting through him. 'Give him back!'

'What's the matter, Nekton?' came a familiar voice. 'Lost your little buddy?'

From behind one of the rusty steel tubes stepped a small girl with black hair holding a remote control. Ant and Fontaine knew this pirate girl by the accurate nickname 'Mad' Madeline.

'Madeline! Put that down!' called Fontaine.

'Or what?' shouted Madeline. 'You know, I've never understood what you see in this thing.' She smiled at Jeffrey – at least, Ant thought it was a smile. The little fish frowned at her. 'How about we send him back to the wild?'

She angled the claw so that the Jorange dangled over the Moon Pool.

'You wouldn't!' screamed Ant. 'He's sealed in the tank! He'd sink like a stone and be lost forever!'

'My thoughts exactly. What's he worth, Nektons? How much to stop your friend here from plunging to the bottom of the biggest fish tank in the world?'

Jeffrey looked through the glass of the Jorange at Ant, his tiny eyes pleading.

Mad Madeline began to lower the claw down, but before Ant could say anything, another – deeper – voice came from behind them.

'MADELINE!' it bellowed. 'There you are! You're needed on deck, my girl. What in the seven seas are you doing down here playing with these lousy plankton?'

The large figure of Captain Hammerhead emerged from the shadows. As he stepped into the light he rippled his muscles and Ant was nearly blinded by his dazzling gold rings.

Ant and Fontaine exchanged a look, shaking their heads in disbelief.

'Hey!' said Fontaine, scowling at him. Captain Hammerhead may have been a beefy, bearded, tattooed pirate, but at that moment Ant thought that his sister was the scarier one. 'We've outsmarted you many times before and we can do it again!'

To prove her point, Fontaine pushed

Madeline and grabbed at the controls of the mechanical arm.

'Hey, stop that!' Madeline snarled, but she was too late. Fontaine hit a release button and Ant caught the Jorange as it dropped. Madeline lunged to grab the controls, but Fontaine managed to hit the button marked 'hatch release' before Madeline wrestled them back. The hatch at the bottom of the Moon Pool slowly opened.

'Are you OK, Jeffrey?' said Ant. Jeffrey bobbed in his tank, his expression as tranquil as ever. 'Look what you did! Now he's stressed! Who do you filthy pirates think you are anyway, using a trawling net? This area is protected by the WOA as an area of scientific importance!' said Ant to the two of them.

But Captain Hammerhead wasn't listening. He strode forwards, pushing past Ant, his eyes fixed on one thing only: the Rover.

Ant followed the line of the captain's

gaze and suddenly realised what was so interesting. The Circlotron was still sitting in the footwell of the cockpit! The captain stared at the mysterious orb and Ant felt a shudder of unease. Why hadn't he put it back in his room? It was possibly the second most important Lemurian discovery they had ever made, and he had brought it straight on to a pirate sub!

Thankfully, Fontaine spied the Circlotron and Ant's worried expression. She stepped in front of Captain Hammerhead, shielding the Rover from him.

'Yeah, what's up with the ridiculously huge net?' she asked.

For a second Captain Hammerhead looked flustered at being told off, but then seemed to remember that he was a huge, fearsome pirate. He stepped up to Fontaine and she gulped with nerves.

'My boat, my business,' he growled. 'And I'll

ask the questions, if you don't mind. Now, how about you Nektons? Made any nice *discoveries* lately? Anything valuable?'

His eyes flitted to the Rover and he grinned, showing his large white teeth.

'Um, Ant?' said Fontaine, not taking her eyes off the captain.

'Uh-huh?' grunted Ant, fastening the Jorange's straps around his shoulders.

'ABANDON SUB!' Fontaine yelled. She turned and raced away from Hammerhead before his meaty hands could grab her, then jumped deftly into the pilot's seat of the Rover, which bobbed on the surface of the Dark Orca's Moon Pool.

Ant ran too – and as he passed a button on the wall that was marked 'FILL BALLASTS', he hit it and leaped into the cockpit to join Fontaine. Deep in the workings of the Dark Orca, the ballast tanks began to take on water, making the sub sink.

'What? No!' bellowed Captain Hammerhead.

'DIVE, DIVE, DIVE!' shouted Fontaine as the craft started to move.

'Fontaine? Is that you?' came the panicked voice of Kaiko over the radio. 'Are you receiving me, over?'

'You're not getting away that easily!' boomed Captain Hammerhead. He snatched the controls to the mechanical arm from his daughter and the claw leaped downwards, grabbing at the Rover's hull like a snapping turtle.

'Hi, Mum!' called Ant. 'Just on our way back! Nothing to worry about!' he fibbed.

The Rover's canopy hissed down, forming a seal around them. Through the Perspex screen, Ant saw Mad Madeline running at them, her eyes wild. She launched herself into the air and landed with a *splat!* on the canopy. She laughed, with her face pressed against the glass, staring in at Ant.

'GO!' he yelled to his sister. Fontaine hit a button and the Rover dropped like a boulder into the ocean. Madeline's laughter dried up and her eyes bulged in panic. One by one, her fingers peeled away from the Rover and then she finally let go, floating back up to the surface of the Dark Orca's Moon Pool. Captain Hammerhead grabbed her with the mechanical claw and hauled her to safety. She called out insults but the Rover was long gone.

Fontaine piloted them swiftly away from the Dark Orca, which, thanks to Ant's quick thinking, was too busy falling to the bottom of the ocean to follow them. Ant patted Jeffrey's Jorange and shielded the Circlotron from sight.

Fontaine noticed what he was doing, even as she kept her gaze fixed on the ocean before them. 'Too late now,' she said grimly. 'I told you it wasn't a good idea to bring that.'

Ant turned his face away and stared out at the ocean. He *hated* it when his sister was right.

*

When they arrived back on the bridge of the Aronnax, they took their seats, exhausted and shaken by their run-in with the pirates.

'You were gone a long time,' said Kaiko. 'Everything OK?'

Ant thought over the conversation on the Dark Orca and decided he couldn't keep it to himself. He told them everything – Mad Madeline's attempt to fish-nap Jeffrey, Captain Hammerhead's appearance and even his sighting of the Circlotron.

'And you're sure he saw it?' asked Will.

'I think so,' said Ant. He knew what his parents were going to say – that he should be more careful around the pirates. He agreed. His encounter with Captain Hammerhead had left him shaken.

'You did well,' said Kaiko. 'And hopefully

you've stopped them from following us! Let's get on with the mission. There's a lot of work to be done.'

The Aronnax's engines fired up again and they sped through the ocean towards the Dragon Hole. Ant couldn't shake the feeling of foreboding. For a few precious weeks, the Circlotron had been his and his alone. He'd worked hard to repair it – scraping off barnacles, polishing the metal, gouging sand out of the etchings. But now things had changed.

Pirates knew about the Circlotron.

CHAPTER FOUR

'**A**pproaching the South China Sea,' said Will. It was morning and he was studying a map that was curled at the edges and must have been hundreds of years old.

'Uh, Dad?' said Fontaine. 'You know we have *new* maps, right? Even state-of-the-art satellite data? You can put the antique ones away.'

Will chuckled to himself.

'True, but these old maps from centuries

ago are pretty detailed. Considering the tools they had, they managed to map the oceans really well.'

Ant looked over his shoulder.

'Cool! It looks like this blue hole was also known as the "Eye of the South China Sea". It even has a warning: *"Here be dragons"*!' he said. Will rolled his eyes.

'Well, maybe they're not *that* accurate,' he admitted. 'But I like to see the oceans the way the ancient mariners saw them.'

'Um, do your maps have *these* on them?' said Kaiko. The crew looked up to the observation screen to see an area of giant underwater mountains, right in their path.

'Seamounts? I can't even see these on our most recent maps,' said Ant with a thrill of excitement. He dashed back to his station to check the monitor. 'They must be brand new. Magma has leaked through the weak ocean floor and cooled to make a mountain.

Look, those round-looking rocks? That's pillow lava! A sure sign of an underwater eruption. Maybe I could quickly hop into the Shadow Knight and investigate while we –'

'Not now, Ant!' chorused his family. He slunk back into his seat.

Kaiko, always cautious, slowed the Aronnax's speed to a crawl.

'At least we know we're on the right track,' she said. 'But now I'm going to have to pilot us through a brand-new mountain range without any maps. Ant, Fontaine, I'll need you both on the sonar to help guide me.'

Ant excitedly called up the sonar display on his monitor – he loved navigating new territories. A crude image of the seamounts ahead of them appeared, the computer creating a visual guide as information bounced back from the high-pitched sound waves that it sent out into the water.

Ant could only just make out the shapes of the mountains; he was concentrating hard and he noticed his hand was shaking.

'Can't we go around them?' Fontaine asked.

'This is the quickest route to the Dragon Hole,' said Kaiko. 'And if we go through the mountain range, we can also gather data on how the sea bed has changed due to the eruptions.' Her voice was tight with determination.

'OK, here we go!' said Ant. He had to focus on the task at hand. If he gave one wrong direction to Kaiko, she could crash the Aronnax! 'Soooo ... port, ten degrees. No, wait! Five degrees! No! Starboard!'

'Ant!' called Will. He waited until Ant looked up at him. 'Breathe. You've got this.'

Ant looked at his father and took one long, deep breath. Then he turned back to the screen.

'All right, sorry. Ten degrees to port.'

'OK,' said Kaiko. She gently adjusted her

steering and the Aronnax obeyed, cruising past the first seamount.

'Twenty degrees to starboard,' said Ant, studying the monitor closely. Kaiko manoeuvred the sub through a new valley. 'And now five degrees port-side.'

'Aye aye, navigator!' she said. 'Good work, son.'

Ant beamed but didn't take his eyes from the screen. The next seamount was coming up. He calmly issued directions. They got into a rhythm and for thirty minutes or more it was all that could be heard on the bridge. Fontaine worked by Ant's side, tracking the navigation and noting down all the new seamounts that they passed.

Finally, they came to the other side of the mountain range. Ant felt the muscles relax in his body.

'We're clear of the seamounts!' said Will. 'Good job, team.'

The Aronnax began to rise as the sea grew more shallow. Ant kept his eyes on the monitors and saw something that made his tummy tingle in excitement. 'Hey, look! It's –'

'The Dragon Hole!' said Fontaine, stealing his thunder. On the sea bed in front of them

was a giant, perfectly round ░
deeper blue than the surrounding ░
steered them as close to the rim o░
as she could, then slowed to a stop.

'Whoa,' said Ant. 'It's so ... deep.'

'Well, *duh*,' said Fontaine. But deep was
the only word for it. Even from inside the
Aronnax, Ant felt dizzy peering down at the
drop in front of them. It was like looking over
the edge of a cliff.

Suddenly from behind them there came
a deep rumble that travelled through the
entire sub.

'An eruption!' said Will. 'Quick, seismic
sensors on screen!'

Kaiko tapped some keys and a computer-
generated layout of the area popped up on
the monitors. Small, pulsating icons began
to flash around the seamounts they had
just passed. Then the icons, flashing red,
got closer and closer to the area where the

Nektons had stopped. The tremors shook up the coloured stones in the bottom of poor Jeffrey's tank.

'Did you feel that?' said Ant, as the tremors died away and the flashing icons on the map disappeared. 'That was a real, live volcanic eruption!'

'Yeah, but a little too close for my liking,' said Fontaine. 'I like my eruptions far away in the distance. Preferably when I'm watching them on TV.'

Ant looked over the map of the area.

'Maybe the Dragon Hole was once a volcano?' he said. 'It kind of looks like one. Dormant of course.'

'That's good thinking, Ant, but it's more likely to be an ancient sinkhole,' said Kaiko.

'Commander Pyrosome was right to be concerned,' said Will, peering at a screen. 'With those eruptions getting closer to the Dragon Hole each time, there's a real danger that the next huge explosion could be right next to the rim.'

'But that's awful!' said Ant. Even Jeffrey looked worried. 'That could be disastrous for all the organisms that exist down there. Whole new scientific discoveries could be lost forever!'

'Then we'd better get to work,' said Kaiko. 'The eruptions could already be poisoning the hole.' She brought up a diagram of the blue pool on the screen for them all to see. 'Usually, there is a layer of hydrogen sulphide that sits deep down in a blue hole. It's a nasty acid that is produced by bacteria living in the water.' She spoke in a quiet voice, talking herself through a line of scientific logic as she worked out what was happening in the Dragon Hole.

It was always fascinating for Ant to watch his mother's mind at work. 'If the volcanic eruptions are disturbing the water, the acid could be killing the sea life in there.'

Ant and Fontaine looked at each other, wondering what this meant. Kaiko looked up at them, her eyebrows furrowed as though she were coming to a decision. Then she gave a curt nod.

'Guys, I'm going to need you to go out there and gather some samples.'

'Yes!' shouted Ant and Fontaine together as they jumped up in excitment. Fontaine dashed off the bridge ahead of her brother.

'Race you!' she called over her shoulder, laughing.

CHAPTER FIVE

'I'm hoping this is going to earn me a *ton* of extra allowance,' said Ant. He was piloting the Shadow Knight through the ocean towards the rim of the Dragon Hole. 'Are you OK in there, Jeffrey?' he asked. Jeffrey was held in a small tank in the belly of the Shadow Knight. He looked up at Ant and gave him a fishy wink. Ant glanced over to see his sister moving alongside him in the White Knight.

It was larger than Ant's Shadow Knight and able to dive to the very deepest part of the ocean – the Mariana Trench – but Ant's was sleeker and faster. Will was following close behind in the Mag Knight, the heaviest of their underwater exploration Knights. The Mag Knight was large and yellow, looking more like it belonged on a construction site.

'Remember, we only need to collect a sample from every ten metres from the rim of the Dragon Hole and then from the hole itself. Let's get this done and get back on board,' he advised. 'It's probably safe, but we shouldn't take any chances.'

Fontaine began to fill a test tube with seawater, but Ant was enraptured by the blue hole. He had never seen the sea that sort of colour: a blue so deep you could get lost in it.

A loud beeping noise made Ant jump. It was coming through his headset.

'There's a fault on my Knight,' came Fontaine's voice over the radio link-up. 'It says that one of the air canisters isn't working. It's probably nothing. I'll just –'

'We're taking no chances, remember?' said Will. He swam over to Fontaine and looked at her suit. 'We're going back on board. Kaiko, are you receiving me?'

'Yes, Will,' said Kaiko on the radio. 'What's your status?'

'Fault detected on the White Knight. Coming aboard.'

Ant started back to the Aronnax, followed by Fontaine, with Will bringing up the rear. He wanted to explore the blue hole more, but he knew the rules: safety first. He swung back around to check on Fontaine.

'Hey, Fontaine, do you think it's a fault in the computer, or –' He froze when he saw his sister's face. 'Dad! Fontaine's in trouble!'

'I don' feel s'gooood ...' slurred Fontaine.

She blinked and wobbled in the water, fighting back dizziness.

Ant sped over and saw her panicked expression up close. He felt his heart hammering in his chest as he floated face-to-face with his sister.

Will scooped Fontaine up and powered through the water towards the Aronnax. 'I've got her, Ant. Moving as fast as I can!' he shouted over the headset.

Ant followed and felt something rumble, a vibration shaking the sea bed.

'Um, Dad? Did you feel that?' he called. 'It might be another eruption!'

'Then let's hurry,' said Will. There was still the danger of not getting to the Aronnax in time, so Will used all the Mag Knight's power to drive them through the water and up into the sub's Moon Pool.

The mechanical arms helped them on to the side of the pool and Will quickly freed

Fontaine from the White Knight. She fell limply into his arms as he shouted through the headset to Kaiko.

'Prepare the sickbay,' he called. 'I'm bringing her up!'

Ant pressed the button that opened the hood of his Shadow Knight and he found himself staring out of a porthole into the water. A shoal of fish zoomed past, seemingly fleeing the blue hole. Had they been spooked by the vibrations? Peering into the deep, he spotted something. Something odd. He froze.

'What. Is. That?' he muttered.

Coming from the direction of the Dragon Hole, two orbs moved across the sea bed. They looked like yellow eyes above a pair of flaring nostrils. Eyes that locked on to Ant's for a moment. It was like looking deep into the soul of a giant ... He gave an involuntary shiver. What was it?

He shook his head clear, wondering if he had been starved of oxygen too. *Maybe I'm hallucinating.* He looked back down, but the pair of bloodshot eyes had gone.

'Hmm. Globules of lava, maybe?' he murmured. He started to unstrap himself from his Knight. He had more pressing things to worry about, like getting Fontaine back to health.

Will was at the door with Fontaine in his arms.

'Ant, come on!' he called.

'I'm coming!'

But as soon as he spoke, a giant tremor shook the Aronnax. The hood of Ant's Knight slammed shut, trapping him back inside. Panic surged through him as the Aronnax continued to judder. He looked down into the Moon Pool, and saw ... something.

Something huge.

Swimming underneath them was a giant

sea creature, something even Ant's rampant imagination could never have conjured.

'I wasn't hallucinating!' he whispered.

A second wave of tremors rocked the submarine. The mechanical arms at the side of the Moon Pool let the Shadow Knight slip from their grasp. Suddenly Ant was plunging down into the water.

'Ant! No!' yelled Will.

But Ant hardly registered his father's voice. He was already gone, and could feel himself sinking down into the ocean and into the path of the giant sea creature. But what kind of creature had eyes as huge and menacing as that?

CHAPTER SIX

'Ant! Are you OK?' Will's voice carried over the link. It came through loud and clear inside the helmet of the Shadow Knight. Ant forced himself to slow his breathing. Panicking wouldn't help anyone. He took a second before replying.

'I'm OK, Dad!' he called.

'Phew! You had me worried. Get back up here now.'

But that was easier said than done. The nearby magma explosions had disturbed the silt from the sea bed, forcing it to drift upwards in huge clouds of dust and grit that swirled around Ant's Knight. It was like wading through a murky, muddy pond. He couldn't see which way was up, never mind his way back to the Moon Pool.

'Um ... that might take a while ...' he said, turning around in the water for a clue of where to swim. He couldn't see the lights of the sub or the floor of the ocean. The only thing he could make out was ...

'Uh-oh.'

A giant fin cut through the murk of the water. Ant saw it and turned, but it had gone instantly. He turned again and spotted it out of the corner of his eye, getting closer. What was it? A creature of some sort, but what?

A tail appeared through the gloom and swung at him. Thankfully the current pushed him away, and the Shadow Knight careered up through the water.

'Whooooaaaa!' he yelled. He landed with a thud against something and he rested on it while the silt cleared. 'What on earth –?'

Ant looked left and right. He had landed between ... were those *horns*?

'Ant? What's wrong? What's taking you so long?' called Kaiko over the radio.

'I, er, may have a situation down here,' he answered, his voice shaking.

The creature started to move and Ant clung on for his life. He brushed his hands across the mysterious creature's scales, but his hands slid – the scales were slimy and slippery beneath his touch and his fingers came away coated in a thick, gelatinous substance that made him shudder with unease. *What the –?!*

'What's that?' Kaiko asked, but Ant didn't have time to reply. He could feel his Knight start to lift and float away. No! If he floated deeper into that murky cloud, he'd never find his way back to the Aronnax. In desperation, he wedged his fingertips under the edge of a huge scale to hold on.

Instantly, the giant creature started to race through the water so quickly that Ant had no choice but to clasp on and hope for the best! He could feel the animal's huge muscles working beneath his grip as the creature moved swiftly through the ocean like a torpedo.

The silt began to clear as they rose through the water and Ant could now get a sense of which way up he was. He looked down at the creature and his heart leaped as he saw the yellow eyes, the dark green scales and – far too close for comfort – the two rows of teeth, as sharp as needles. If Ant had reached out just half a metre to his left, his arm might have been breakfast for a sea creature.

Despite how terrifying it was to be this close to a lethal set of teeth, Ant's mind couldn't help scrolling through his brain's search history. Hadn't he seen something like this recently during another one of his late-night research sessions?

'It's like the old book in Dad's library! An plesiosaur!' he said aloud. 'Or at least it's a long-long-long-long-looooong lost cousin of the plesiosaur, evolved over millions of years.'

'What are you saying, Ant?' came Kaiko's voice over the radio. He could hear the concern. 'You're breaking up.'

'Mum, I'm riding a sea dragon!' he yelled. 'Woo-hoo! The exploding magma must have scared it out of the Dragon Hole and into the ... Whoa!'

Before Ant could finish what he was saying, the creature shot through the ocean, its pointed nose slicing through the water. It zigzagged left and right, zooming through kelp forests and coral reefs. Ant clung on – it was going faster than his Shadow Knight could and if he fell off now he would get seriously hurt. The sea dragon was bucking like a bronco and would not calm down.

'Uh-oh!'

Up ahead through the murkiness of the silt, Ant saw a wreck of an old fishing boat covered in seaweed and barnacles. The wreck's mast had collapsed to make an arch – and the sea dragon was heading straight for it! Ant quickly calculated the size of the hole and the size of the creature – there was no way they could make it through!

'Stop! Pull up! Whoa!' he called, to no avail. With seconds to go, Ant ducked down low, hugging the creature tight. They smashed through the hole, the horns of the dragon protecting Ant from getting a faceful of the mast, which splintered apart, spreading itself over the sea bed.

Ant sat up again, sighed with relief and gulped as the creature swam up, up, up. Its fin propelled it through the water and they breached the ocean surface, leaping out of the sea like a giant dolphin. Ant could feel the adrenalin pounding in his ears as sunlight warmed his face, the round orb of the sun hovering near the horizon.

'Ant, what are you talking about?' said Kaiko, her voice becoming clear once again. 'There are no such things as dragons!'

Ant held on tight as they arced through the air and splashed back down into the water.

'Try telling that to this guy!' he yelled.

Beneath his grip, the creature tossed and turned in distress. Ant didn't think it was because he was riding it – he was so tiny in comparison to the dragon that he wasn't sure it even knew he was there. The creature sped through the water towards the blue hole.

It's going home, thought Ant. The creature swam faster and faster, until Ant could hold on no longer.

'Uh-oh!' he cried out. 'It's been fun, but I think the ride's over!'

He hurled himself clear at the last moment, activating the Knight's engines and steering himself away to safety. They were clear of the silt cloud now and he'd be able to find his way back to the Aronnax. He looked back just in time to see the giant fin disappear from view into the dark heart of the hole. Looking up, he could see the belly of the sub floating above him and he sighed with relief.

'Incredible!' he said. He steered the Shadow Knight towards the Aronnax, beaming with delight. Exhilaration coursed through him. 'Hey, Jeffrey. Just think! We can now officially – or *almost* officially – call ourselves Dragon Riders! Woo-hoo!'

CHAPTER 7

Back on the bridge of the Aronnax, Ant joined his family for an emergency meeting. Fontaine was back to full health after her blackout. An hour on oxygen in the sickbay was all it took to get her vital readings looking normal again.

Ant told them all about his ride of a lifetime on the back of the 'sea dragon'. He didn't leave out any details – he even added some more,

as well as sound effects and mimes to bring the whole story to life. After all, it wasn't every day that he got to ride a creature like that. Why not make the most of it?

'A dragon, Ant? Seriously?' said Fontaine, her arms folded.

'Seriously!' he insisted. 'Just ask Jeffrey.'

Jeffrey, safely back in his tank, stared blankly.

'Jeffrey is a *fish*, Ant!'

'Hey! He's still part of the family!'

'Is not!'

'Then how come he's at the family meeting?'

'Enough!' shouted Kaiko. 'Let's just stick with the facts and say that Ant discovered a *creature*. Most likely it was living in the blue hole and was disturbed by the eruptions.'

'What I don't get is that it was huge. How have we never seen one like it before?' said Fontaine.

Ant's hand shot up. 'Ooh! I know! I know!' he shouted. 'Blue holes are also called "insular ecosystems". That means they contain a whole array of life, and it would be possible for a creature – like the dragon – to live inside the hole and never need to come out. It would have all the food it needs.'

'Very good, Ant,' said Kaiko.

Will stared at the map of the area on the observation screen. The location of each eruption was highlighted in red.

'So that's fact number one,' he said. 'Fact number two: the magma eruptions are definitely getting closer and closer to the blue hole as the crust of the Earth gets thinner.'

'If they get any closer, it could disrupt all the organisms in the Dragon Hole. It could kill tons of sea life!' said Ant. He thought back to the dragon, and how agitated it had been. 'I can't believe we found a real, living dinosaur, and it could soon be doomed to extinction. Again!'

'Well, technically the plesiosaur isn't a dinosaur – it's a reptile,' Will reminded him.

'Cool!' said Ant.

'Ahem! Let's not forget fact number three:

the water may be poisoned,' said Fontaine.

'Correction: the water *is* poisoned,' said Kaiko, leaning over a monitor. 'The results from the first sample you took just came through. It's full of sulphur, which is turning to acid. Look.'

She pulled out a small sheet of steel, tipped a drop of the sample from a test tube on to the metal, and they all watched in horror as it fizzed and hissed, giving off a foul stench as it ate through the steel.

'Wait, is that what happened to the air canisters on my Knight?' asked Fontaine. 'No wonder I ran out of oxygen! Thank goodness it didn't happen to Dad and Ant's canisters too.'

'If it can do that to metal, what's it like for all the wildlife out there?' said Will.

Ant froze, and the image of the dragon came back into his mind. Those scales ... covered in that thick layer of slime. The bloodshot yellow eyes. Maybe the dragon (because Ant was definitely calling it a dragon, no matter what his family said) had been affected by the sulphur. That was why it was looking sick and why it was behaving so strangely.

'We have to stop the eruptions!' he said. 'We can't let them harm the dragon any more.'

'Ant, for the thousandth time, there are no such things as dragons,' sighed Fontaine.

'OK, reptile. Fine!' Ant smiled. 'If we can't

decide what it is, we'll call it ... Brian!'

'This really isn't the point,' said Kaiko. 'We need to resolve this situation. Isn't that why Commander Pyrosome asked us to come here?'

'*Told* us to come here,' Ant said.

Kaiko rolled her eyes. 'The commander doesn't get to tell us what to do. But look, are we agreed? We need to save this poor creature!'

'Agreed,' said Will. 'Now, how are we going to save him?'

Will stared at the maps and charts and went into what Ant called 'Deep Thought'. His father was able to concentrate so deeply that he could blot out all the sounds around him. It was incredible to watch. Eventually he snapped out of it and looked at his family.

'Simple. The explosions are caused by the magma getting too hot for the crust of the Earth. So we need to cool it down!' he said.

'If we get a large drill and make holes in the crust, we can siphon off heat from the magma. Then "Brian" can be saved.'

'Yes! Some of the heat will be released outside the blue hole, but with some luck we can keep it from erupting inside,' said Kaiko.

Fontaine and Ant exchanged a confused glance.

'Wait, that's the *simple* plan?' said Ant. 'So where are we going to get a huge drill?'

'Well, we have a drill for collecting rock samples, but I doubt it'll be big enough,' said Kaiko. 'We're going to have to ask for help.'

CHAPTER 8

The observation screen hissed and crackled as a video call stuttered into life. Suddenly a face appeared with a smile, glasses, a shock of red hair and a matching red beard.

'Greetings, Nektons!' Professor Fiction was stationed at the Nekton secret headquarters in the South Pacific, thousands of miles away. He was their chief science adviser and inventor. 'To what do I owe this delightful correspondence?'

'We're trying to save a dragon!' said Ant before anyone else could get a word in.

'*Still* not a dragon, Ant!' corrected Fontaine.

'OK! We're trying to save a *Brian*.'

'Professor,' interrupted Kaiko, 'we need a way of drilling down through a shallow section of the Earth's crust. We need to release heat from a build-up of magma.'

The professor stroked his chin for a few moments before jabbing a finger in the air. Clearly a light bulb had gone off in his head.

'Well, it's funny you should ask,' he said brightly. 'The answer is actually under your very feet.'

Ant frowned. 'Do you mean my shoes?'

The professor shook his head, grinning. 'There is a large drill in the bowels of the Aronnax which would be perfect for your mission,' he said. 'You'll be able to locate it in area 7B of the cargo hold.'

'Wait, we have a drill you never told us about?' said Will, looking offended. 'Why didn't you tell us about this before?'

Professor Fiction shrugged.

'It's always good to have something up your sleeve for emergencies!' he said, before brushing over the subject. 'Now, you'll be able to control the drill from the bridge. But be careful! That's a razor-sharp, diamond-tipped tungsten drill bit. It could drill through the hull of the Aronnax if you don't aim it right.' A map of the Dragon Hole replaced Professor Fiction's face on the screen.

'With the data available, I calculate that you should drill around the sinkhole here, here and here,' he said. Yellow crosses appeared on the map, surrounding the sinkhole. 'Not too close though!' warned the professor. 'If you drill within a metre of the sinkhole the limestone may crumble in and trap, er, "Brian" forever. You'll need someone on the ground to make sure that the holes are being drilled in the right places – there's a lot of coral out there that will need protecting.'

Ant stuck his hand in the air.

'I'll go!' he yelled. Will looked over, frowning.

'I don't know, Ant. It looks pretty dangerous, especially with all that magma,' he said.

Professor Fiction appeared back on screen. A crease furrowed his brow. 'I wasn't joking when I said you'd need to be careful,' he warned. 'This exercise will need the utmost precision, or you'll do more harm than good. Ant, can you guide the drill exactly?'

For a moment, Ant felt a shadow of doubt. But he quickly shoved the thought away.

'Come on, you guys. It *has* to be me!'

he said. 'I'm small and fast, and Brian already knows me! If he sees me working he won't be too alarmed.'

'I don't want you anywhere near that creature,' Kaiko said in a low voice. 'He dragged you above surface level, remember?'

'He didn't drag me anywhere. I was holding on. Without him, I'd have been lost in the ocean.' Ant kept his voice soft and reasonable; he didn't want this to turn into an argument now. Not when he could be out there, guiding a giant drill!

Will and Kaiko looked at each other. Ant often wondered if they were telepathic, as they were often able to have a full conversation with one look. He crossed his fingers behind his back.

'OK,' said Kaiko eventually. 'But if you begin to experience any faults on your Knight like the one Fontaine had, you head back to us immediately, no matter what. Promise?'

Ant crossed his heart and saluted.

'Promise!'

*

Ten minutes later, Ant was suited up in the Shadow Knight. Jeffrey swam in his tiny tank in the belly of the Knight, looking more than a little worried.

'Hey, buddy, everything's going to be all right!' Ant said, trying to calm his friend.

'Yeah,' said Fontaine. 'Nothing to worry about. Just going out to the bottom of the ocean to drill holes into a volcanic area where a giant prehistoric sea monster is living.'

'Not helping, Fontaine. Not helping,' said Ant. He leaned in to whisper to Jeffrey. *'Don't listen to her – she's trying to get into your head!'*

Will controlled the claw from the comfort of his seat on the bridge, monitoring it on the big screen. Once he had found the drill in the vast cargo hold, the claw automatically attached itself.

'Wish me luck!' said Ant. He grabbed hold of the drill and Will lowered him down into the water.

A security camera on the hull captured the moment that the drill, gleaming silver and glinting in the light, moved out into the water with Ant swimming by its side. Kaiko thrust the controls forward so that the sub dived down to the sea bed, scattering a school of fish.

'OK, we're ten metres above the sea floor.'

'Ant, I'll be controlling the power to the drill,' said Will. 'I need you to guide the drill bit to the sea floor and tell me when to turn it on. Try not to hit any coral or get too close to the sinkhole.'

Ant took hold of the drill with the Shadow Knight's arms and guided it down to an area of the sea bed where they could make a hole.

'OK, power on!' he called. The drill started to spin and a column of bubbles rose up

from it as the razor-sharp tip came closer and closer to the sea bed. Ant suddenly spotted it veer down towards a piece of coral and yelled out.

'STOP,' he said, beginning to panic. 'I need to move the drill to the east. Wait, no, west! Wait –'

'Ant,' said Will's voice quietly but firmly over the radio. 'Take a breath. You –'

'I know, Dad,' said Ant with a smile. He took a deep breath and let it out slowly. 'I've got this.' Calmer now, he checked the drill, moving it away from the coral.

The tip punctured the rock and sent up a flurry of dust that dispersed through the water. A shoal of angelfish bobbed at a safe distance, watching proceedings. *They must wonder what on earth is going on*, Ant thought, laughing silently He quickly glanced around for any sign of Brian, but he must have been hiding.

Ant focused his attention back on the drill. It bore down into the rock for a few more minutes. Ant couldn't see much of what was going on as the clouds of silt and rock dust grew bigger, but suddenly the drill broke through the crust and a burst of hot air released a bulging column of bubbles that rose up to the surface.

'Nailed it!' said Ant. 'Now the next one.'

The second hole was easier, and Ant kept his nerve. Soon they had another column of bubbles as compressed gas and magma safely escaped without causing an explosion. They were doing it!

Ant could feel the heat of the magma even through the protective suit of his Knight.

'How are the gas levels, Mum?' asked Ant. Kaiko took a moment to answer as she checked the read-outs on her instruments.

'Yes! They're diminishing,' she said. There was a note of relief in her voice. 'Soon the sulphur levels should be back to normal. Just one more hole to drill.'

Ant helped them guide the drill to its final position and Will began to lower it.

'Great ... good ... easy now,' said Ant, talking his father through every centimetre of the way. Suddenly a shoal of fish zoomed past him, spooked by the giant drill. There were hundreds of them, and his view of the drill was blocked. 'Whoa!'

Ant waved his arms, trying to bat away the fish like they were a swarm of bees. They moved away and he dived towards the drill. In the few seconds he had been unable to see it, the drill had drifted nearly half a metre off course. It was close to piercing the side of the sinkhole, spelling disaster!

'Whoa! Stop, stop, STOP!'

'What's the matter?' asked Will.

'Stop the drill!' Ant yelled. Will hit the emergency 'off' button and the drill slowed, spinning to a stop. Ant surveyed the damage. He had taken the edge off a small part of coral and created a dent in the rock. He had almost failed in his task, but he took a deep breath, corrected it, and guided the drill down to create the final heat vent. 'Hit it, Dad!' The heat escaped, rising up to the surface, and Ant patted the drill.

'We're done!' he called. 'You can retract now.'

The ocean was eerily silent after all the noise of the drilling.

'Toxicity levels are dropping already! It's working!' said Kaiko.

'Yes! So Brian's going to be OK?' asked Ant.

'I think so, Ant. I think so.'

'Um, Ant? I'm picking up something on sonar. Something big!' said Fontaine.

Ant turned to the Dragon Hole and peered into the darkness. A giant pair of eyes and a snout emerged from the sinkhole, watching.

'Hi, Brian,' Ant whispered.

'Ant! Get out of there!' screamed Kaiko.

But Ant stayed completely still. The creature's eyes were already less yellow. He found himself drifting over to look more closely.

'Ant! Back on board. Now!' called Will.

'Guys, it's OK,' Ant whispered. 'He's not going to attack.'

Brian emerged into the open. His smooth body moved more gracefully, not jerking and nervous like it had been before. Ant held his ground.

'Hey, Brian,' he said softly. 'You're going to get better now.' He smiled.

Brian circled Ant, keeping a giant, bulbous eye on him all the time. He was getting the measure of him. Then he swam forwards gently to touch his snout against the Shadow Knight. He squeezed his eyes shut in a way that Ant could have sworn meant 'thank you'.

'Whoa,' Ant whispered. 'Amazing!'

Brian's eyes snapped back open and the two of them gazed at each other for a long moment. Ant knew how lucky he was to be this close to such a rare inhabitant of the ocean. The creature turned and disappeared into the blue hole. Ant was ready to head home, but then the creature's snout appeared out of the Dragon Hole again.

'Are you ... are you waiting for me?' asked Ant. Brian gave no answer, but instead headed into the dark blue void of the hole. Ant powered the Shadow Knight forwards until he was peering down into the depths. Could he follow Brian? It would be safer than taking the Aronnax down the hole, he reasoned, and the water was much safer now the magma pressure had released.

Maybe I should just make sure Brian gets home safely ... he thought, secretly dying to explore the blue hole.

He swam over the edge of the hole and followed Brian down, down, down into the darkness. The lights on the Shadow Knight automatically lit up. He passed columns of coral that clung to the sides of the rock, and strange-looking fish that darted out of Brian's way. It was like falling down the rabbit-hole towards Wonderland.

The creature led him down, further into the depths of the blue hole, unworried that Ant was following him. Brian slowed and swam into a cave opening, back in his lair once more.

'Is this your home? Is this what you wanted to show me?' asked Ant. Brian turned in the mouth of the cave and looked at him again. Ant knew what the look meant. 'Yeah. Goodbye, Brian.'

The shining yellow eyes backed into the cave and Ant looked up at the creature's home.

'Oh! Oh, whoa!' he cried. He angled his headlights up to illuminate the rock around the mouth of the cave. He couldn't believe his eyes. Framing the cave perfectly were stone columns, and carved into the rock was an ancient, worn-down Lemurian symbol. It was hard to tell what it would have been when it was first made, but Ant had an idea.

'It's a dragon!' Ant frowned, trying to make out the carving. But then there was a rumble from the Knight's tank as the Circlotron began to judder into life. 'What's happening, Jeffrey?'

The fish seemed to shrug his tiny shoulders when a symbol began to glow on the rim of the Circlotron. Ant looked from the Circlotron to the cave, finally understanding what he was seeing.

'It's a child and a tiny mountain!' he said to himself. The etching and the glowing symbol matched exactly. 'They're Lemurian symbols. They have to be! And that means the ancient Lemurians must have been here.'

'*Fzzt* – Ant? Are you there?' came a distorted voice over the radio. It was Will. 'Come in, Ant, come in!'

Ant stared up at the symbol. It was time to head home.

'Yeah, I'm here,' he said. He engaged the Knight's engines and swam up towards the surface. 'And you guys won't believe what I found!'

CHAPTER NINE

After Ant returned to the Aronnax, everyone went to the bridge to report back to Commander Pyrosome on a video call.

'It goes without saying that the WOA is extremely grateful for your efforts,' said Pyrosome's giant head on the screen.

'Does it, though?' said Ant. He smiled cheekily. 'I feel like you should actually *say it*, at least once.'

The commander glared at him and tried to form the words in her mouth. She was used to receiving thanks, not giving it.

'Thank you,' she muttered. Kaiko gave a small smile. 'The puzzle of the Dragon Hole has been solved and the area around the Eye of the South China Sea is stable,' the commander said. 'Anything else to report?'

The Nektons looked at each other. They had agreed before they called the commander that they would not mention the amazing discovery they had made. The last thing that Brian needed now was a research team from the Worldwide Oceanic Association poking their noses into his home.

'Nope,' said Ant.

Commander Pyrosome squinted at the screen.

'You're sure? There's nothing else?' she pried. The Nektons all shook their heads. 'Anything you're not telling me?'

'Of course not, Commander,' said Will. 'Was there something else you wanted?'

Commander Pyrosome frowned with suspicion.

'No. That is all.'

She snapped off the call without so much as a 'See you later'.

'Phew! Nice work, everyone. I thought one of us would crack under the pressure for sure!' said Ant. Suddenly Will leaped up and clapped his hands. 'Let's have a celebratory meal!'

'Really?' asked Ant.

'Really! There's so much to discuss – I mean, we've just discovered a real, living kind-of-dinosaur!'

They all walked to the galley and found snacks and cakes in the cupboards. Will raised a glass of juice and proposed a toast.

'To Brian!' he cheered, and everyone raised their glasses.

'Do you think Brian will be OK?' asked Ant.

He thought back to the huge creature with his kind yellow eyes in his deep, dark cave.

'He's a giant, ugly sea monster,' said Fontaine, messing with her little brother. 'Who's going to argue with him?'

Ant didn't dignify that with a response, but instead stole the slice of cake from her plate and ran out of the galley.

'Hey!' she yelled. 'Dad, tell him!'

But Ant was long gone. He raced down the corridor and back to the bridge, where he sat down next to the Ephemychron, an ancient navigational computer covered in rune markings that the Lemurians built to help them sail the Earth. Ant and his family had pieced it together from parts they had found around the world, and now only Ant was able to operate it.

Munching on Fontaine's cake, he pulled out the Circlotron and placed it next to the Ephemychron. Sure enough, the etchings on the Circlotron's rim looked like the symbols on the Ephemychron. *Definitely* Lemurian.

He ran his finger across the dragon symbol on the Circlotron. *Just like Brian*, he thought. Next to the dragon was the picture of a stick-figure child and one of a mountain – the one that had glowed into life by the cave. He picked it up to look closer and, as he cupped the Circlotron in his open palm, he felt a buzz of energy as it came alive again in his hands.

'I didn't even switch it on!' he said to himself. But he remembered it coming to life on its own earlier. Clearly whatever Will had turned on with his DIY key, it looked as though the Circlotron was back to full power. It just needed to be held by ... 'Me!' Ant cried, as understanding dawned.

A white beam shot into the sky, drawing the line along the celestial equator again.

At the same time, the dragon, child and mountain symbols on the Circlotron's rim lit up.

'Cool!' The beam of light wavered. It flashed across the sky, then settled as it started to arc over to the east of the Aronnax.

'Ant? What's going on?' said his dad's voice from behind him. The rest of the family had gathered in the open doorway, watching Ant and the Circlotron. Will stepped further into the room and watched, going into 'Deep Thought' again.

'Look, Dad,' said Ant, holding out the Circlotron. 'It's a dragon symbol – just like Brian!'

'Hmmm. And a child and a mountain to the east. What could that be?' Will's hand froze, holding a half-eaten slice of cake in mid-air. He looked to Kaiko and they did their 'psychic conversation' again.

'Of course! Child of the Mountain,' said Will. 'That's the Arafura Sea!'

'Huh?' said Ant.

'The name Arafura comes from an indigenous term which translates as "Child of the Mountain",' Will explained.

Ant raced to his station, still balancing the Circlotron in his hand, and checked on a map.

'Yes! That's to the east of here. Well, the *south*-east but, y'know, close enough,' he said. 'It's where the light of the Circlotron is pointing. It's guiding us!'

Ant looked back round at his family.

'Are you thinking what I think you're thinking?' said Will.

Ant shrugged. 'I think we know where we need to go next,' he said. 'There's something here that needs investigating. The Circlotron is virtually *ordering* us to go and explore the Arafura Sea.'

'But what's in the Arafura Sea?' asked Fontaine. 'Why are we being sent there?'

'We won't know until we get there,' said Ant, nearly bursting with excitement. He carefully placed the Circlotron on a desk and the white beam shrank back as the orb's buzz of energy faded away.

Ant stared at his treasure, found on the ocean floor. 'The Circlotron could be tracking a route the Lemurians once travelled. The rim is covered in Lemurian symbols, which kind of suggests that they have something to do with all this. What do you say?'

Will and Kaiko grinned. Even Fontaine gave a shrug of agreement.

Ant looked over at Jeffrey, who was swimming in tight, excited circles around his fishbowl, clearly ready for his next adventure.

'All crew on deck,' said Kaiko, sitting down in the pilot's seat.

'Yes!' shouted Ant, punching the air with his fist. As they set off, he cast one last glance at the night sky. What else would they discover if they followed the Circlotron's guiding light? There was only one way to find out.

'Setting sail!' called Kaiko. The Aronnax picked up speed and headed out into the ocean towards the next adventure. Ant peered out at the Dragon Hole for one last time. Brian was out there, somewhere. But ahead of them? Who knew what waited for them in ...

THE SEA IS DEEP AND FULL OF SECRETS

TURN OVER TO FIND OUT MORE!

PROLOGUE

A tall, burly man walked with a rolling gait to the edge of the harbour. The brass buttons on his pea coat glittered in the rays of the setting sun. Waves broke gently against the sea wall, and a fishing boat bobbed in the water next to a landing stage.

Two people in overalls were crouched over the boat. One was attaching some sort of device to the front of the vessel. The other wore a welder's mask and was soldering two large metal plates together. A shower of sparks flew from the torch.

'Ahoy there!' called the burly man.

The figure in the mask straightened up and looked round sharply. A hand went up to raise the mask, revealing the face of a young woman with flushed cheeks, short dark hair and intense green eyes.

'Captain Hammerhead. About time.' The young woman climbed a set of iron steps to where the pirate stood. He gazed down at the boat. The other worker was still busily fixing some piece of tech to the prow. 'Making some improvements, Edwina?'

Edwina shrugged. 'When you don't have the Worldwide Oceanic Association behind you, you have to be resourceful, right?'

Captain Hammerhead gave a hoarse, guttural laugh. 'You said it. Ducking and diving, that's us.' His laughter stopped as quickly as it had begun and he fixed her with a level stare. 'Got the necessary?'

Edwina delved into her pocket and brought out a grubby envelope. Captain Hammerhead snatched it and ripped it open, riffling his thumb through the notes of money inside. 'Seems to be all there,' he grunted.

'Now hand over the goods,' said Edwina. 'And this better be worth it.'

The Dark Orca's captain laughed. 'Oh, it's worth it, all right.' He took a small electronic tablet from inside his coat, touched the screen and showed her the display.

There was an image of a tarnished brown orb, small enough to fit perfectly in the palm of her hand. Around its centre was a protruding ring covered in mysterious symbols. It looked indescribably old.

Edwina snatched the tablet and stared. 'The Esgis! I thought it was lost forever!'

'Well, it ain't. It was aboard my sub not long

ago. But I never got my hands on it.'

Edwina looked up at him, eyes burning. 'Who has it, then?'

'The Nektons. They've got it on board the Aronnax. You're the only one who knows, apart from me.'

Edwina handed back the tablet and called down to the man who was still working on the boat. 'Hurry up and finish installing that, d'you hear? I need that boat, and fast.' She turned back to the captain. 'Where are the Nektons now?'

Captain Hammerhead held out a hand. 'Extra information costs money.'

Edwina narrowed her eyes. 'You've had everything you're getting.'

He grinned, revealing pearly white teeth. 'Can't blame a pirate for trying. All right, we intercepted their signal. They're headed for the Arafura Sea.'

Edwina gave a sudden high-pitched laugh.

'Good – not too far from here. I hear there's a cyclone heading that way. I can use it to my advantage.' She took out a tablet of her own and keyed in a code, her fingers a blur. Then, with an air of triumph, she held out the screen to the captain. He saw the WOA logo and underneath it the words: SATELLITE FEED TO ARONNAX – STRICTLY CONFIDENTIAL.

'I've hacked into the WOA feed – now I can intercept their messages. The Nektons won't be getting any warnings about the cyclone!'

'So they're heading straight into the storm?'

'And I'm going after them,' Edwina said, gazing out to sea.

Captain Hammerhead gave a low, appreciative whistle. 'Ain't no stoppin' you, is there?'

'I'd do anything to get hold of the Esgis,' she said, leaping down to the boat. '*Anything!*'

CHAPTER ONE

Ant peeled the wrapping from the fortune cookie and snapped it open. A shower of crumbs fell on the table as he pulled out the slip of paper.

'"Today is the day to show someone you care,"' he read out loud. 'Yeah, maybe there's something in that. Maybe I should show my feelings more.'

He began to walk towards his big sister,

Fontaine, arms spread wide, mouth puckered up for a kiss.

'No way – urgh!' Fontaine scampered round to the other side of the table. 'Keep away from me!'

Ant carried on walking straight past her and picked up the Jorange – the portable tank that his pet fish, Jeffrey, swam around in. He planted a kiss on the side of the fish tank, and Jeffrey swam up, and appeared to press his tiny lips to the glass.

'Thank goodness for that!' said Fontaine. 'Like, narrow escape.'

'It wasn't that narrow,' Ant assured her.

'Ha ha, very funny,' said Fontaine, folding her arms. 'Anyway, the fortune cookie said show *someone* you care. Jeffrey isn't a person, he's just ... well, just a fish!"

Ant clamped his hands to the sides of the tank. 'Hey, watch what you're saying, Jeffrey has feelings, you know! He's not *just* anything – he's the best fish in the whole wide ocean!' He gazed down at his tiny friend. 'Aren't you, Jeffrey?'

'He's not in the ocean, he's in your home-made aquarium,' said Fontaine. 'He may be the best fish in there. Just about.'

Ant glared at Fontaine as his parents, Will and Kaiko, exchanged a smile. The Nekton family were gathered on the bridge of the Aronnax as it powered its way through the ocean. Kaiko had steered it down to a depth of a thousand metres, heading towards the Arafura Sea. They had stopped off at Hong Kong to refuel and replenish their supplies, and Ant had taken the opportunity to stock up on fortune cookies. Big time. The table was littered with cookie crumbs and empty wrappers, and there was still a sizeable pyramid of unopened cookies, containing slivers of paper waiting to tell their fortunes.

'Go on, your turn,' Ant said.

'Oh, all right.' Fontaine unwrapped another cookie, broke it apart and unfolded the message. '"Life's journey is always an adventure,"' she read aloud.

'They got that right!' said Kaiko, looking up from the screen on her console. 'I don't know how or why this happened but – our satellite connection is down!'

'I don't call that an adventure!' Ant said. 'An adventure should have, like, sharks and dragons and pirates and sea monsters!'

'Maybe they'll put in an appearance later,' said Kaiko. 'But right now this is quite enough to deal with.'

'Is it such a big deal though?' Will asked in a reassuring voice. He leaned over her to take a look at the screen. 'We can still manage – we have the charts, and you're a great pilot, Kaiko.'

A soft bleeping noise, like someone hitting a xylophone with a padded stick, rang through the bridge. 'Ah, that means we've entered a new area. We're in the Celebes Sea now,' Kaiko said.

Will pored over one of his charts on the map table. 'Just under five hundred kilometres till we hit the Arafura Sea.'

'Arafura,' Ant said dreamily. 'Isn't that a great name? "Child of the Mountain", that's what it means.'

'Yeah, but what does *that* mean?' said Fontaine. 'Does anybody know?'

Will looked up, a curious frown on his face.

'I don't know yet,' said Ant. 'But I'll find out. Mysteries are made to be solved!'

He went over to the display stand on the map table, where the Ephemychron lived. Once a navigational tool of the ancient Lemurian people, it was a greenish copper orb covered with mysterious symbols. Beside the Ephemychron stood another, smaller orb of tarnished brown. The Circlotron. Together, they looked like a planet and its moon, thought Ant. The Circlotron had a ring around its middle, covered in more Lemurian etchings. Ant had discovered it during a dive in a kelp forest, and had lovingly restored it.

He'd found a way of switching on the Circlotron so that it shot a beam of light into the night sky, picking out the celestial equator. The first time it had happened was so cool! Admittedly, Ant still wasn't quite sure what the device was actually *for*, but he had an idea that it was tracing a route. A route that the Nektons were supposed to follow. To where … ? It was Ant's mission to find out.

He carefully took the Circlotron from its holder on the map table. It was the size of a cricket ball – small enough to balance in the palm of his hand. He often placed it inside his Jorange, so he could take it on his travels if needed. Plus Jeffrey was a great guard-fish.

Now he held the Circlotron in his hands. He was the only person who could control it and when he held it, a beam of light would shoot out. There were other times when some of the etchings on the rim had lit up. The etching of the dragon had taken them to a lair where Ant had found a hidden cave. There, another symbol had lit up on the Circlotron – of a child and mountain. It matched a symbol carved into the cave and Ant felt certain the Circlotron was guiding them along the equator towards the Arafura Sea, named after the Child of the Mountain.

'Not now, Ant!' said his mother, as if she had eyes in the back of her head. 'I'm trying to navigate and I don't want beams of light shooting all over the bridge, thank you very much!' She peered more closely at the screen in front of her. 'Something funny's going on here. Looks like there's an object – what is it, a fish? – moving about under the hull.'

Will came to stand beside her. 'Pretty big fish,' he commented.

'Oh wow, d'you think it's a great white shark?' said Ant excitedly. 'Or a giant oarfish? Or ... or ... ?'

'Calm down, Ant,' Kaiko said. 'I can't get a proper look at it. It's too close to the hull.'

Ant came running over to the console and squeezed in beside his mother. Fontaine followed. A dark, blurred shape was moving on the screen. It grew bigger and the next moment there was a *bump* that rocked the Aronnax.

'It hit us!' said Fontaine.

'Whatever creature's down there, it's a bold one,' Will said.

'Maybe it's a sea serpent!' Ant said. He just couldn't stop imagining sea creatures. 'Or ... or ... a sea goat!'

'A *what*?' said Fontaine, giving him a withering glance.

'A sea goat – I've been studying the stars. Did you know there's a whole constellation named after the sea goat – Capricornus!'

'Yes, Ant, but it's not an actual creature,' Fontaine said patiently. 'I suppose you'll be saying there's a giant scorpion in the sea next, just because there's a constellation named after that.'

'Who knows what's down there in the deep?' Ant challenged her. 'We didn't expect to find a dragon – until we found one.'

'It was an evolved plesiosaur, not a dragon,' said Fontaine.

'Well, we didn't expect to find an plesiosaur!' They'd encountered the ancient creature living in a cave at the blue hole in the South China Sea. Ant had even ridden on its back. He was so excited, he'd christened the ancient creature – um – Brian.

'Anyway, we didn't expect to find Brian,

but we did!' he reminded his sister. She wasn't going to win this argument!

Before Fontaine could reply there was another *bump*. The ship lurched more violently than before. Kaiko and Will exchanged a concerned look.

'Do you think we should go out and chase it away, whatever it is?' said Will.

'I'm sure it doesn't mean to harm us,' Kaiko said, sounding less than one hundred per cent sure. Then she brightened. 'Anyway, look, it's going!'

Sure enough, the shape on the screen was getting smaller.

Ant ran to the window and peered out into the ocean, hoping to catch a glimpse of the creature. He thought he saw a black, streamlined shape moving swiftly away from the Aronnax – but before he could focus on it properly, it had disappeared.

'Whew,' said Will. 'Alarm over.'

Kaiko shook out her shoulders and stretched her neck. 'You guys can take a break if you like. We're on course, and everything's under control now.'

'Sure?'

'I know you've been dying to go to your library and consult your books, ever since Fontaine asked Ant why the Arafura Sea is called Child of the Mountain!'

Will grinned. 'Am I really that transparent?' He was already walking towards the library.

Ant and Fontaine followed. Ant wondered what idea had occurred to his dad. Perhaps he'd suddenly remembered something buried in one of his old books, another clue that would guide them in their search for the lost city of the ancient Lemurians!

LOOK OUT FOR MORE
ADVENTURES FROM

THE DEEP

OUT NOW!

THE SEA IS FULL OF SECRETS!

Join the Nektons on their daring underwater adventures with more books all about

NEVER SEEN ON SCREEN!

THE DEEP: STICKER ACTIVITY BOOK

The Nekton family are on a mission to shine light on the darkest extremes of the ocean. Packed with super submersibles, astonishing sea creatures and breathtaking Lemurian mysteries, this sticker activity book will take you on all the amazing aquatic adventures of The Deep!

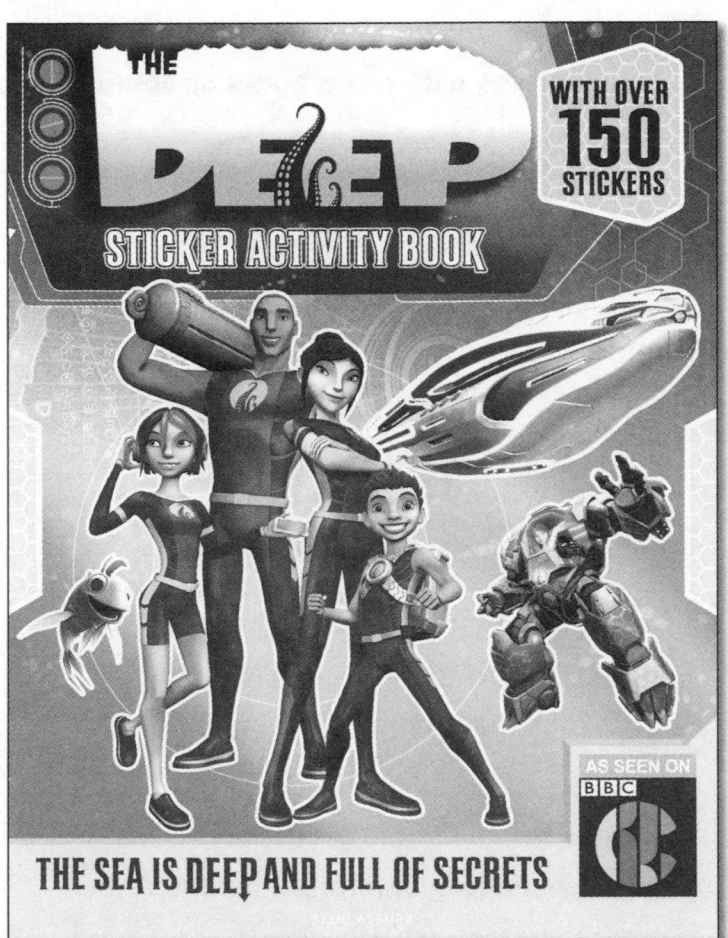

THE SEA IS FULL OF SECRETS!

Join the Nektons on their daring underwater
adventures with more books all about

NEVER SEEN ON SCREEN!

THE DEEP:
THE OFFICIAL HANDBOOK

Explore the depths of the captivating world
of The Deep with this official handbook,
the must-have companion to the hit TV
series! It's packed with never-seen-before
material, including in-depth profiles of all
your favourite characters and behind-the-
scenes stories that have inspired episodes.
Discover the secrets of Lemuria and watch
out for pirates along the way!

TURN OVER FOR SOME FUN GAMES!

CORAL AND CURRENTS

Fontaine is roaming the ocean in the White Knight, searching for a rare species of hermit crab. Now it's time to return to the Aronnax. Can you help her find a way through this rocky reef? Kaiko is worried – Fontaine's air supply is running low!

THE WHITE KNIGHT

The White Knight is a single-person, armoured diving suit. It can reach places underwater that would be too difficult for a normal diver to explore.

THE SEA IS THE KEY

The Nektons are determined to find the sunken city of Lemuria, even if it takes years! All they have to guide them are a few ancient artefacts. Study these four Lemurian symbols. The same sequence only appears once on the tablet below. Can you find it?

PROTEUS

Proteus is the leader of the Guardians, a secret society who have existed for thousands of years. They are tasked with protecting Lemuria and its treasures.

Got it right? Proteus will be impressed! Stick the Guardian in here.

7

NEKTON VERSUS NEKTON!

Ant, Fontaine, Kaiko and Will are putting the Knights through their paces! They've set up a race in the waters around a deserted island. Who will win the challenge? Stick in the contestants, then trace their routes, adding up the numbers along the trail.

The Knight with the highest total is the winner!

THE WHITE KNIGHT
Diver: Fontaine

THE SWAMP KNIGHT
Diver: Kaiko

11

2

5

9

13

6

7

9

10

1

3

THE **DEEP** STICKER ACTIVITY BOOK

WITH OVER 150 STICKERS

AS SEEN ON BBC

THE SEA IS DEEP AND FULL OF SECRETS

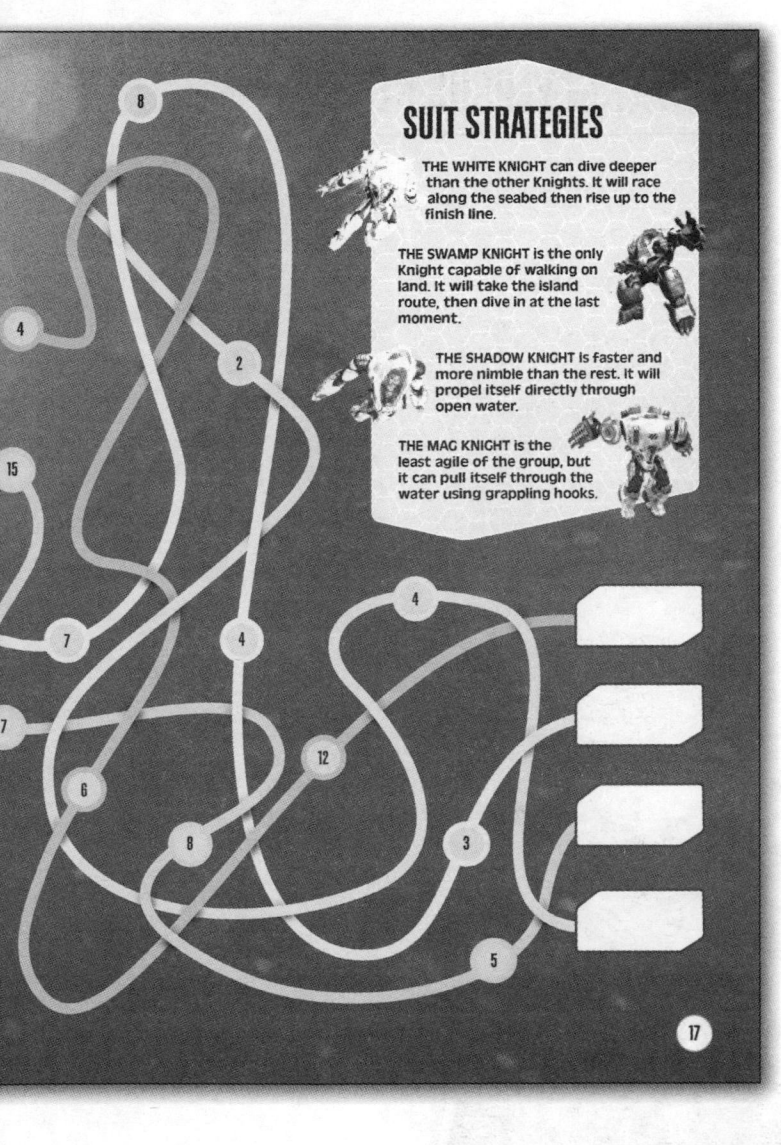

SUIT STRATEGIES

THE WHITE KNIGHT can dive deeper than the other Knights. It will race along the seabed then rise up to the finish line.

THE SWAMP KNIGHT is the only Knight capable of walking on land. It will take the island route, then dive in at the last moment.

THE SHADOW KNIGHT is faster and more nimble than the rest. It will propel itself directly through open water.

THE MAG KNIGHT is the least agile of the group, but it can pull itself through the water using grappling hooks.

MISS THE ABYSS

Ant is a first-class swimmer, but right now he's totally out of his depth! He needs to carry a heavy load back to the Aronnax, without falling into this sea hole. Kaiko and Will are waiting in the Rover. If they move any closer, they could sink in, too.

LOOK OUT FOR MORE ADVENTURES FROM

COMING IN 2019!